My Best Friend, Bob

For my mum, with much love – G. R.

First published 2003 by Macmillan Children's Books
This edition published 2004 by Macmillan Children's Books
a division of Macmillan Publishers Limited
20 New Wharf Road, London N1 9RR
Basingstoke and Oxford
Associated companies throughout the world
www.panmacmillan.com

ISBN 978-0-333-96085-1

Text and Illustration copyright © Georgie Ripper 2003

Moral rights asserted.

9 8

A CIP catalogue record for this book is available from the British Library.

Printed in China

My Best Friend, Bob

Written and illustrated by

GEORGIE RIPPER

MACMILLAN CHILDREN'S BOOKS

Brian the guinea pig lived in a nice comfy
cage in Pete's Pet Palace, with his best friend Bob.

Brian had short, shiny fur which he was very
proud of. Bob had long, tufty fur which he didn't
really think about all that much.

The two little guinea pigs spent

their days doing what guinea pigs do best –

eating, sleeping and playing 'I Spy'.

Brian was terribly good at 'I Spy', and almost always won with clever words like 'budgerigar' and 'dog food'.

One day, Brian and Bob were busy playing when a little boy walked into the shop.

"I spy with my little eye," said Bob, but before he could finish, the little boy reached into the cage and picked him up.

"I want this one," the boy said. "I shall call him Fluffy."

Brian watched as Bob was put into a cardboard box with holes in the lid. He just had time to wave goodbye, and Bob was gone.

Suddenly the cage felt very big and empty.

"Oh dear," sighed Brian. "I shall miss Bob." And he trundled off to find a peanut to cheer himself up.

But he didn't cheer up at all.

In fact, every day Brian missed Bob more and more,
and every day he felt more and more miserable.

Then, one day, Brian was sitting in his cage
feeling very glum, when he noticed an
old man peering down at him.

The man picked him up
and smiled. "He's just
what I was looking
for," he said and
he put Brian into
a box.

At first Brian was excited. "Maybe there will be other guinea pigs in my new home," he said to himself.

He began to whistle and felt much more cheerful.

But that evening, he found himself all alone, without so much as an earwig for company. Brian sighed. He wished he was back in Pete's Pet Palace. At least he could chat to the goldfish there.

"I wonder what's happened to my best friend Bob," whispered Brian. "He's probably forgotten all about me by now." He wiped away a tear and curled up in the straw.

The next morning, Brian hadn't even opened his eyes when he felt his box being lifted up.

"What's happening now?" he grumbled. But he didn't really care. Things couldn't get much worse than they already were.

He drifted back to sleep, dreaming of Pete's Pet Palace and winning a peanut-throwing contest with Bob.

A little while later, Brian was woken by a buzz
of excited voices outside his box.

"Oh, bother," he said crossly.

"Can't I at least have some peace

and quiet?" Then suddenly the lid

was lifted off and bright light

streamed into the box.

Brian looked up to see a
little boy smiling down at him.
He sleepily wondered if he had seen
the boy somewhere before.

The boy picked
Brian up and gave
him the biggest
hug he'd ever had.

"Oh, thank you,
Grandad," he said
happily. "He's
just what I
wanted. I shall
call him Snuffles."

The little boy put Brian into his new hutch.

Brian stretched out and sniffed the air.

"That's funny," he said, and he sniffed

the air again.

As Brian watched, a pile of hay in the corner

started to move, and all of a sudden . . .

BRIAN!

Brian was so excited to see Bob that he thought
he might just burst with happiness.

That evening, sitting together in their hutch
playing 'I Spy', the two little guinea pigs had almost
forgotten they had ever been apart. "I spy with
my little eye," said Bob, "something beginning with P . . ."

But Brian was already fast asleep.

ALSO WRITTEN AND ILLUSTRATED BY
GEORGIE RIPPER:

Little Brown Bushrat